P9-DWI-156

Beast Quest®

DevorA
THE DEATH FISH

BY ADAM BLADE

ORCHARD

With special thanks to Tabitha Jones

To Mylo Rich, hero of the future

www.beastquest.co.uk

ORCHARD BOOKS

First published in Great Britain in 2021 by The Watts Publishing Group

1 3 5 7 9 10 8 6 4 2

Text © Beast Quest Limited 2021
Cover and inside illustrations by Steve Sims
© Beast Quest Limited 2021

Beast Quest is a registered trademark of Beast Quest Limited
Series created by Beast Quest Limited, London

The moral rights of the author and illustrator have been asserted.
All characters and events in this publication, other than those clearly in the public domain,
are fictitious and any resemblance to real persons, living or dead, is purely coincidental.

All rights reserved.
No part of this publication may be reproduced, stored in a retrieval system, or transmitted, in any form
or by any means, without the prior permission in writing of the publisher, nor be otherwise circulated in
any form of binding or cover other than that in which it is published and without a similar condition
including this condition being imposed on the subsequent purchaser.

A CIP catalogue record for this book is available from the British Library.

ISBN 978 1 40836 529 8

Printed in Great Britain

The paper and board used in this book are made from wood from responsible sources

Orchard Books
An imprint of Hachette Children's Group
Part of The Watts Publishing Group Limited
Carmelite House, 50 Victoria Embankment, London EC4Y 0DZ

An Hachette UK Company
www.hachette.co.uk
www.hachettechildrens.co.uk

Welcome to the world of Beast Quest!

Tom was once an ordinary village boy, until he travelled to the City, met King Hugo and discovered his destiny. Now he is the Master of the Beasts, sworn to defend Avantia and its people against Evil. Tom draws on the might of the magical Golden Armour, and is protected by powerful tokens granted to him by the Good Beasts of Avantia. Together with his loyal companion Elenna, Tom is always ready to visit new lands and tackle the enemies of the realm.

While there's blood in his veins, Tom will never give up the Quest…

There are special gold coins to
collect in this book. You will earn
one coin for every chapter you read.

Find out what to do with your coins
at the end of the book.

CONTENTS

For a time, I was the most powerful Master of the Beasts who ever walked this land. A royal prince. A courageous hero. People chanted my name.

But at the peak of my fame, it was taken from me by cowards.

For almost three centuries my spirit has wandered the realms. In ghostly form, I have searched for the one magical token that will bring me back.

And now I have found it, Avantia will pay for her treachery.

Only a fool would stand in my path.

Karadin

THE HAND OF KARADIN

Tom bit his lip to keep from crying out as Elenna wrapped bandages around one of his injured hands. "If only I could find some willow bark to help heal the wound," Elenna said as she crouched beside the charred tree stump on which Tom slouched. She cast her eyes about doubtfully, and Tom followed her gaze. The forest was charred, and the bitter smell of smoke still lingered from the many fires Gorog had started.

Silver stood nearby, alert and watchful, his eyes glowing like twin moons against the smouldering remnants of the Forest of Fear. Beyond Elenna's wolf, Tom's stallion, Storm, pawed at the black earth, clearly as anxious to be off as Tom was. *We have to stop Karadin before he raises another Beast!*

Tom had been badly burned fighting Gorog, the deadly varkule-Beast raised by the Evil shadow ghost, Karadin. The healing powers of Epos's talon had stopped the blisters weeping, but Tom's palms were still red-raw and hurt as badly as ever.

"How does that feel?" Elenna asked, as she finished wrapping the second bandage.

"It's much better," he said through gritted teeth.

"Liar," said Elenna.

Tom managed a smile. "We need to get going."

As Tom spoke, a swirl of mist appeared at Elenna's shoulder, quickly resolving into a familiar, ghostly form. It was the spirit of Prince Loris, Karadin's younger brother. The two princes, sons of an ancient king called Mandor, had once shared the role of Master of the Beasts in Avantia. Karadin had returned from the dead after his skeleton hand was uncovered at King Hugo's Palace. Loris had appeared too, and was now helping Tom and Elenna on their Quest to stop Karadin taking Avantia's throne.

"My brother is already far ahead of us," Loris said, his pale, translucent face etched with worry. "But before you set off in pursuit, there are things you must know."

Tom nodded. "We had better be quick," he said.

Loris closed his eyes and drew his hands together. He stayed silent

so long, Tom was about to protest –
This is no time for prayer! – when
suddenly, Elenna swayed and closed
her eyes, and Tom's own eyelids
became impossibly heavy. He
couldn't keep them open… But, as
they fell shut, instead of darkness,
he was met with the clear, cold
light of a winter's day. He could
hear a high wind whistling, but his
body felt numb. Even the pain of
his burned hands had dulled to a
distant throb.

"What is this?" Elenna asked, her
voice sounding thin and far away.

"After my brother killed me, I
followed him in my ghost form,"
Loris explained. "You are now seeing

what I once did…"

Turning his attention to the scene before him, Tom saw a crescent of snow-capped mountains jutting into the sky, each peak as sharp and white as a wolf's tooth. Near the jagged summits, nestled on a rocky plateau, sat a small village of squat stone huts. The biggest building, a rectangular hall, stood in a courtyard at the heart of the village. Tom recognised the place.

"That's Colton!" he said. It was the highest town in Avantia, and barely seemed to have changed since Loris's time.

"Yes," Loris said. "Now watch."

As Tom looked closer, he saw a

broad-shouldered knight dressed in full armour marching up a narrow path towards the mountain village, his dark cloak billowing behind him. In one hand, the warrior carried a broadsword, and in the other, a shield bearing the sigil of two crossed blades. A gleaming ring on his finger caught the sun, sending out rainbow sparks.

"Karadin!" Elenna said. Tom knew that she was right. The

ghost they had encountered still wore the same snake-shaped ring on his skeleton hand – it was this that allowed him to raise Beasts.

"Once my father learned that my brother had killed me," Loris went on, "he vowed to stop Karadin. However, he knew he could not defeat Karadin himself, so instead, he set a trap. My father sent his most feared warrior north to Colton, then made sure that stories of a Beast rampaging in the village reached my brother's ears. Karadin headed there immediately, expecting an easy victory. Instead, he found an ambush."

Right on cue, Tom's vision shifted,

swooping in close to the village of Colton just as Karadin reached the empty market square and stopped before the town hall's heavy doors. He rapped on the wood with a fist.

"I come to defeat a Beast!" he bellowed.

The doors flew open, and a huge brute of a man stepped out. Clad in leather and chainmail, he stood a head taller than any warrior Tom had ever faced, and twice as broad. Bushy brows almost hid his fierce blue eyes and a red beard brushed his barrel chest. In one meaty hand, he brandished an axe few men could lift; in the other was an immense longsword. He smiled broadly,

showing yellow stumps of teeth.

"I am no Beast!" the huge man boomed in a voice like an avalanche. "And no man has ever defeated me! Put down your weapons and give me your ring. You will be spared, though you will spend the rest of your days in King Mandor's dungeon."

Karadin hefted his own sword. "Never," he shrieked, the veins on his neck bulging in rage. "I came here to kill a Beast, but I can kill a treacherous dog instead!"

The warrior let out a furious roar, then lunged, swinging his sword. Karadin threw up his shield, deflecting the blow, and jabbed his own weapon towards his opponent. His blade was met with a powerful swipe of the warrior's axe. The blow should have driven the smaller man to his knees, but Tom was amazed to see Karadin simply parry the strike.

Then he remembered that the magic ring Karadin wore contained the essence of every Beast he had defeated. It gave the Evil prince strength no human should possess.

The mountains echoed with the ring of steel on steel as a mighty battle ensued. Though Mandor's champion wielded his huge weapons with skill and superhuman strength, he was no match for Karadin. The prince deflected every blow, and answered with a jab or thrust of his own.

Before long, the bearded warrior was panting hard and bleeding from numerous cuts to his torso and arms, while Karadin looked as fresh as if he were taking a stroll.

Suddenly, a group of villagers rushed from behind the town hall, attacking Karadin with clubs and knives. In the chaos that followed,

Tom saw a flash of steel, followed by a spray of red droplets. The throng of villagers parted, and Karadin staggered back, clutching the bloody stump where his sword hand had once been. In the silence, the village chieftain darted forward and snatched up Karadin's bloody hand, snapping it shut in a metal box.

"So that's how he lost his hand," Elenna said.

Karadin staggered back away from the villagers, a burning hatred in his eyes. "You will regret this!" he hissed. "I will return, and I will have my revenge, on Colton, on my father…on any man who dares stand between me and my birthright, the throne of Avantia!"

Tom's vision began to blur and dim, the image dissolving into darkness. He opened his eyes to find himself staring into the sooty shadows of the Forest of Fear. Loris's insubstantial form was just about visible, and he was shaking his head sadly.

"I never thought my brother would

wage a war with death itself," the ghost said.

"It's not a fight we can let him win!" Elenna said, balling her fists.

Tom let out a heavy sigh. The horrible, burning throb of his hands had surged back, sapping his strength. "But if even death didn't stop Karadin, how can we?" he asked. "What was it Karadin said after we killed Gorog? Something about fighting against him only making him stronger?"

Elenna nodded. "This is going to be a tough Quest. Maybe our toughest yet. But we can't give up. The safety of Avantia depends on us!"

Tom drew himself up to stand tall,

and squared his shoulders. "You're right," he said. "While there's blood in my veins, Avantia will never be ruled by Evil! Somehow, I will find a way to stop Karadin!" Tom turned to Loris. "I take it Karadin's heading to Colton?" he said.

The ghost nodded gravely. "My brother once defeated a terrible Beast that lurked in the lake high up there," he said. "Now he will be looking to raise that Beast and take revenge on the village."

"Then let's go!" Tom said.

STAMPEDE

As Tom and Elenna rode out from
the gloomy shadows of the Forest
of Fear and on to the vast Central
Plains, the sun was just rising above
the clouds, casting a gold and rosy
glow across the open grassland.
Scouting ahead, Silver picked up
his pace, bounding through the long
grass with his ears back and his

tail held high. Though Tom's head ached with weariness and his burns throbbed, the sight of the old wolf stretching his legs made him smile.

Elenna, who had taken Storm's reins to save Tom's injured hands, chuckled from her seat in front of him. "Silver's like a pup again in all this space!" she said. But then, glancing around at the wide expanse of grassland, Elenna shuddered. "We're too exposed," she said. "Is there no other route to Colton? Some way with more shelter where we can't be seen?"

Tom shook his head. "None that I know of. But there's no reason for Karadin to stop here. And anyway, this is Tagus's territory. He looks after the herds and everything that lives on these plains. He won't let any harm befall us."

Elenna nodded. "I hope you're right!"

They rode on at a steady trot and, with the Forest of Fear behind them, made swift progress over the rolling grassland. As the daylight strengthened, warming Tom's tired muscles, his spirits began to lift.

"We'll make Colton by noon at this rate!" he said. But as he spoke, they reached the top of a gentle rise to find Silver waiting for them, standing stock still with his ears pricked and his hackles raised.

Elenna pulled Storm to a halt at her wolf's side. "What is it, boy?" she asked. The wolf growled softly, and Storm tossed his head, letting out an anxious snort. Tom froze, his breath catching in his throat. He could feel a deep, jolting vibration rising through his stallion's muscular legs and into his own. And now they had stopped, the jumbled clatter of hoofbeats reached him from across the plains. Hundreds of hoofbeats, getting louder by the moment!

Scanning the horizon, Tom spotted a cloud of churning dust; a dark splotch, spreading like an inkblot. His skin prickled with dread. A huge herd of cattle was speeding towards them, out of control. "Stampede!" he cried.

Elenna cursed. "Silver! Stay close!" she called to her wolf, then yanked Storm's reins, wheeling him around into a gallop. Silver kept pace with Storm, staying right beside them. The thud of hoofbeats ringing in his ears, Tom glanced back at the stampeding cattle. *This is all wrong!*

Where's Tagus? The centaur-Beast was one of Tom's most trusted friends. He never normally let the cattle run wild. Elenna craned low over Storm's neck, urging the stallion away from the advancing herd. Tom looked back to see the cattle fanning out as they drew close, a deadly tide surging forwards at impossible speed. Storm's hooves flew over the grassland, but he was already weary from a morning's ride. Tom knew they had no chance.

Clinging to the saddle with his knees, Tom fumbled for the horseshoe token in his shield – a gift from Tagus. He called on the horseshoe's magical speed to help

Storm, but the token felt cold and dead. Storm struggled on, his sides heaving, no faster than before. Tom tore the bandage from one hand with his teeth, but the token didn't even respond to his bare skin.

Churning dust and the thunder of hooves filled the air. Looking back, all Tom could see was a mass of rolling eyes and tossing horns. Storm whinnied in panic, stretching his neck, his mane and tail streaming behind him.

"Hold tight!" Elenna cried. Tom clung to her waist as she tugged the reins, bringing Storm to a sudden halt. Tom's teeth clashed together and agony seared through his injured hands. He feared he would yank Elenna from the saddle, but grunting with effort, she somehow kept her seat. The herd closed around them, snorting and bellowing, a river of tossing horns and muscled flesh. Dust burned Tom's eyes and throat. Storm whinnied with fear as the ground shook like an earthquake. Silver crouched at Storm's side.

Then suddenly, the stampeding herd was past, speeding away over the open grassland. Tom let out a shuddering breath. He could feel Elenna shaking all over. Storm's eyes were wild with terror. At his side, Silver was panting hard, his fur clogged with dirt. But they were unharmed. *We did it!*

"Nice riding!" Tom told Elenna.

"Thanks," she said weakly. "But what was it you were saying about Tagus?"

Tom's elation vanished as he remembered how the Good Beast's token had failed him. "Something's very wrong," Tom said. "Tagus's horseshoe didn't respond when I called on it." Tom showed Elenna his shield. The horseshoe, along with more than half of his other tokens, looked strangely dull and grey.

"What does it mean?" she asked him.

Tom shook his head. "I don't know.

I'll try to ask Tagus."

Tom put his hand to the red jewel in his belt that allowed him to speak with the Beasts.

Tagus! Tom called with his mind. *Where are you? Why are you not guarding the plains?*

In response, he heard the thud of mighty hooves along with a bellowing snort. *Who are you to question me?* the horse-man said. *I have a new Master now!*

Elenna suddenly grabbed Tom's arm. "Tom, look!"

Tom looked up to see the muscled form of the centaur cantering towards them over the plains with Karadin on his back. The Evil ghost still looked shadowy and dim, but he was more solid than Tom had seen him yet.

"Karadin has enchanted Tagus," Elenna said.

Tom clenched his teeth. "The Good Beasts must be confused," he said. "They can sense

two Masters of the Beasts, which would explain why my tokens aren't working."

As he drew closer, Tagus lowered his massive, shaggy head, his eyes blazing with fury. Then he brandished his mighty sword. Sitting astride the centaur's back, Karadin grinned, his own weapon raised.

"We have to get out of here," Elenna said. "I'm sorry, Storm!" She drove her heels into the stallion's sides, and he leapt into a run, speeding away from Tagus. But, glancing back, Tom could see the centaur hurtling towards them, gaining by the moment. It was hopeless.

"No!" he said. "We can't outrun Tagus. We have to face him."

Elenna hesitated, then nodded.

With a deft tug at the reins, she wheeled Storm around, just as Tagus reached them.

"Duck!" Tom cried, pushing Elenna down as he too lowered his head. Tagus's huge sword swept over them so close that Tom felt it part the air. He managed to lift his shield just in time to deflect a second swipe from Karadin.

"After them! Quick!" Tom cried as the centaur clattered past. Elenna yanked the reins once more, bringing Storm around to gallop after the horse-man. Tagus turned too, but Storm had a head start on him and closed on the Beast from the side.

Scowling with fury, Karadin

lifted his sword for another strike, and Tom suddenly noticed that the shadow man had become almost opaque. *If he's solid, he can be hurt! This is my chance!* Raising his shield before him, Tom let out a roar and leapt from the saddle, throwing his full weight against Karadin. With a strangled yelp, the Evil prince toppled from Tagus's back. Tom almost went with him, but managed to grab a handful of the centaur's thick mane to anchor himself. He threw an arm around the horseman's broad chest.

Tagus, it's me! Tom cried, using the power of his red jewel. *It's Tom! Not just your master, but your friend!*

Tagus bellowed, his hooves
wheeling in the air as he reared up
and almost threw Tom off.

Tom held tight, pressing his face
against the centaur's muscular back.
Calm! he ordered the Beast. *Be calm,
my friend! All is well!*

Gradually, the horse-man's wild

bucking slowed. He let out a final puzzled snort, then fell still.

Nearby, Karadin was already on his feet, his lips drawn back in a grimace of hatred. "Don't think that you can win," he spat. "I am stronger than I have ever been. If you follow me to the Northern Mountains, if you try and stand between me and my birthright, the frozen heights will be your grave!"

"You will never take the throne of Avantia!" Tom cried. But then he growled in frustration. Karadin had vanished in a swirl of smoke, leaving Tom still clinging to Tagus's back, staring at empty grassland.

3

CASTOR'S LAKE

Tom released his grip on Tagus. *Are you well, my friend?* he asked.

Tagus shook his head. *I... I am so sorry, Tom...* The Good Beast's voice was filled with sorrow and regret. *I should not have followed the shadow-master. I should have known better. I remember him from long ago. The cruel prince, intent only on his own glory. But it is my destiny to do as a Master of the Beasts bids me. In my weakness, I was unable to resist.*

Tom slid from Tagus's back and gently rested his sore hand against the horse-man's flank. *It was not your fault*, he told him. *Do not fear. Karadin will not control you again. While there is blood in my veins, I will rid Avantia of him once and for all.*

As the heat of the day began to fade, the Northern Mountains loomed above Tom and Elenna, dark and ominous in the failing light. Gazing up, Tom saw that snow and ice still clung to the jagged peaks.

Elenna shivered, drawing her cloak closer about her. "How can people survive in such a place?" she asked.

"They make a living as quarrymen and goatherds," Tom answered. "But it is a harsh and dangerous existence – even without a Beast to contend with. The path upwards is narrow. We'll have to leave Storm here."

As Tom and Elenna dismounted, Tom caught a movement from the corner of his eye and turned to see Loris appear, faint and shimmering, like frozen breath hanging in the air. "Colton is not far now," he said, his voice so weak Tom had to strain his ears. "Unfortunately, I will not be able to lead you there. Because Karadin and I were once dual Masters of the Beasts, our spirits are entwined. As he grows more powerful, my own strength wanes. I believe you will need my guidance yet, so I must depart to conserve my energy. But beware. My brother blames this place for the loss of his powers. He will be intent on revenge."

"What about the Beast in the lake?" Elenna said. "Can you tell us more?" Loris didn't reply. His insubstantial form was already swirling like mist. An instant later, he had vanished.

Tom gazed up at the ice-capped summits towering above them. A cold knot of dread squeezed his gut. "Whatever Beast lives up there, it's sure to be as cruel and deadly as the mountains themselves," he said. "And Karadin may already be working his Evil. We had better hurry."

As Tom and Elenna made their way up the craggy, winding path, Silver scouted ahead, his nose to the ground and his hackles raised. The way was

steep, and the higher they went, the thinner the air became. Tom soon found himself growing light-headed. The pain from his wounded hands nagged at him constantly, and he couldn't focus. Each time his mind drifted, angry whispers crowded his thoughts. Through he couldn't make out the words, he knew the voices. It was the Good Beasts, speaking through the power of his red jewel. *They must be disturbed by Karadin's presence*...Tom tried to push the discontented voices from his mind, but they filled him with dread, weighing him down, making every step harder.

The sun dropped lower as they

climbed and the air became icy, numbing Tom's fingers and toes. Even Elenna was slowing, her back bent low and her breath laboured. The only signs of life were scraggy goats huddled on narrow ledges and, as twilight fell, the faint glimmer of campfires scattered in the heights – groups of goatherds or quarrymen resting, taking their evening meal.

Eventually, they reached a low stone wall: the outskirts of Colton itself. A sudden wave of nausea hit Tom, making him sway on his feet. Elenna put out a hand to support him.

"What's wrong?" she asked.

"It's the Beasts…" Tom said. "Karadin's presence makes them

restless. And it's almost as if I can feel him too, in the back of my mind... He is close."

Tom shuddered, letting the hideous feeling of wrongness guide him. The dizzying nausea grew steadily stronger as they skirted around Colton, the stone buildings of the town only visible by the glow of lights at their windows and doors. Silver trotted at Elenna's side now, glancing warily into the shadows, his ears alert for any sound. The still air was bitingly cold, but instead of cooling the pain of Tom's burns, it just added a new layer of agony. His boot hit a ridge in the rock and he almost fell. Elenna gave him her arm, and he took it gratefully.

As they stumbled on, Tom began to worry that he had taken a wrong turn; but finally, with the village below them, Silver let out a warning growl. Tom followed the wolf's gaze to a narrow ravine ahead. He could feel what the wolf sensed: a strange, crackling energy in the cold air, like the threat of a thunderstorm. He and Elenna exchanged wary glances, then readied their weapons and set off again. When they reached the top of the rocky gully, they both stopped dead and gasped. Ahead lay a wide, frozen lake, gleaming silver-blue beneath the evening sky. In the centre of the lake, Karadin stood with his back to them, his skeleton hand raised and his magical ring pulsing with platinum light.

"He's going to wake another Beast," Elenna said. "Just like he summoned Gorog."

"Not if I reach him first," Tom growled. He tightened his grip on his sword and forced himself to stand tall, despite his pain. "Cover me," he said. Elenna aimed an arrow at the shadow prince as Tom ventured on to the ice, stepping carefully so as not to slip or make a sound. Edging towards Karadin, Tom lifted his sword, ready to strike. But without warning, the Evil prince spun around, his black eyes flashing with hatred.

"You again!" he spat.

"Stop whatever wickedness you are doing and leave this place!" Tom cried.

Karadin let out a short bark of laughter. "What a brave young Master of the Beasts!" he said, his voice dripping with sarcasm. "But they say the line between bravery and stupidity is a fine one. And your bravery is getting in my way! I think it is time *you* left!"

Before Tom could charge, Karadin lifted his hand once more. A gleaming blade of light shot from the ring on his finger, striking the surface of the ice in front of him with a *crack*. Elenna fired her arrow, but it sailed through Karadin's shadow form and clattered on to the ice beyond him.

"I have waited two centuries to take my revenge on Colton!" Karadin cried. "Nothing will get in my way!" A terrible splitting, cracking sound rent the air, echoing through the mountains. Karadin cackled with laughter as the deep ice before his feet shattered, creating a web of fractures that zigzagged towards Tom.

Tom lurched back. *Too late!* The ice beneath him split apart into chunks which pitched and bobbed. Black water welled and lapped at his feet. His stomach flipped as he lost his footing and plummeted...

4

MAROONED

Icy blades of pain stabbed every part
of Tom's body as he plunged into the
freezing water. His muscles clenched
in shock and he had to fight a deadly
urge to gasp. Kicking his arms and
legs, he tried to reach the surface,
but a strong current sucked at him,
dragging him beneath the ice.

Shuddering with cold, Tom drove a

slow, clumsy fist at the pale, frozen ceiling above him. It was like hitting a brick wall. *Stay calm!* he told himself, forcing his rigid muscles to relax, gritting his teeth against the powerful convulsions that gripped him. *I just have to find the hole I fell through.* But suddenly, a strange, croaking, chittering sound started up all around him. It made his flesh creep as if bugs were crawling under his skin. *A Beast?* Peering fearfully through the gloom, he spotted a shifting mass of silvery bodies... *Fish?* They were small, but so numerous they almost seemed to form a solid mass. And they were heading straight towards him! In the half-darkness, Tom made out hollow eyes and pockmarked scales... gaping mouths with needle-sharp teeth. *Piranhas!*

Panic rising, Tom thrashed his arms and legs, trying to push himself away from the deadly shoal, but the fish closed on him, surrounding him. He could hear the tinny chomp of hungry jaws as tiny dagger teeth

nipped and snapped first at his clothes and then, in a hundred needle points of agony, his flesh. *Help!*

Calling on the strength of his golden breastplate, Tom scraped and tore at the creatures, snatching them from his skin, kicking and punching them away. But his magical strength came only in feeble bursts, ebbing and flowing, and his frozen limbs were heavy and stiff. Fear crept into Tom's heart as he realised he couldn't rely on his Golden Armour. At the worst possible moment, its magic was failing him. His lungs felt ready to burst with lack of air. Each time he managed to snatch a set of biting jaws from his body, more took their place... Tom clawed at the fish, thrashing his arms and legs. But it was no use. His own blood billowed all around him, driving the fish into a wilder frenzy.

Desperate for air now and every part of him hurting, Tom looked up just as a shaft of moonlight hit the frozen lake above. He finally saw a break in the ice. *Yes!* Tom kicked towards it, ignoring the biting fish, fighting with every last shred of strength he had to reach the hole. Gripping the jagged edges, Tom heaved, but his bandaged fingers slipped and couldn't get a purchase on the ice. Suddenly, strong hands

grabbed his wrists and tugged.
Elenna! Tom kicked his legs as
his friend pulled, and at last, he
emerged, shivering and bloodied,
on to the ice. Elenna tore a few
stray fish from his tattered clothes
and threw them back as Tom lay
shuddering, catching his breath. He
curled into a ball, hugged himself,
trying to stop the powerful spasms
of cold shooting through his body.

"Thank you!" he said weakly.

"Don't thank me yet," Elenna said,
flashing him a rueful smile. "We're
stranded." Gathering his strength,
Tom pulled himself up and saw that
she was right. Black, choppy water
surrounded them. He and Elenna

were stranded on a floating sheet of ice a long way from any shore. Karadin had vanished and a huge section of the lake had been shattered into bobbing ice floes – the nearest, much too far to jump.

Glancing back the way they had come, Tom spotted Silver pacing up and down on the shore, whining anxiously, unable to find a path to his mistress and unwilling to brave the icy water. Elenna glanced fearfully about them. "What do we do?" she asked. Tom had no answer. And, as he wracked his brains for a plan, a hideous grating, chomping sound started up at his feet. He looked down to see the piranha fish snapping at the edges of their frozen island, gnawing through the ice.

"Get away!" Elenna yelled, jabbing at one with her bow, but the creature snapped at the wood and she snatched her precious weapon back. "Can you jump us to safety?" she asked Tom.

Tom sized up the distance to the nearest ice sheet, then glanced down at the ravenous piranha fish, snapping ever closer. "It's too risky," he said. "My powers aren't working properly, and if we fall in, those things will finish us in a heartbeat."

Elenna frowned. "Not working? How?" she asked.

"I think it's because there are two Masters of the Beasts in the kingdom," Tom said. "Like Tagus, the Golden Armour doesn't know who to serve." Hearing the whispering of the Beasts in the back of his mind, Tom had another idea. "Maybe I can call Arcta. He protects the frozen heights."

"But…what if Arcta is loyal to Karadin now, like Tagus was?"

Elenna asked.

Tom drew a shuddering breath.
His teeth had started chattering so
hard he could barely speak, and his
muscles were locked. He knew he
didn't have long.

"It's a risk we have to take." Tom
put a hand to the red jewel in his
belt and reached for the Good Beast
with his mind.

Arcta! Can you hear me? For a
long, terrible moment, Tom heard
no answer. He pushed away his pain
and weariness and forced himself to
concentrate.

Please, Arcta! I need your help!

This time, Tom felt a flicker of
recognition from the mountain

giant. But it lasted only an instant before it was crowded out by all the other whispers still fighting to be heard in Tom's mind.

"Tom, look!" Elenna cried. Tom glanced down to see the piranha fish had almost reached his toes. He stepped back as far as he could without falling into the lake and started stabbing at the fish with the point of his sword. Elenna drew an arrow from her quiver and did the same.

Together, they jabbed and thrust, barely managing to keep the snapping monsters at bay. As their tiny island of ice diminished, Tom began to lose all hope that Arcta

would come. But finally, after what
felt like a lifetime, Tom heard a
deep, resounding bellow. He looked
up to see Arcta's huge, shaggy form
appear on the far side of the lake.
Tom had never seen a more welcome
sight. With his single red eye, Arcta
quickly took everything in, then
plunged into the freezing water. The
giant cyclops waded towards Tom
and Elenna, easily shoving ice floes
from his path as he went. The Good
Beast was soon submerged almost
to his chest, but he ploughed on,
thrashing his mighty arms to clear a
way through the ice. Tom reached for
the Beast with his mind.

Beware, he told him. *There are*

piranhas in the lake.

Arcta let out a deep, booming chuckle. *Those little fish can't hurt me*, he told Tom. Arcta waded on, finally drawing close to Tom and Elenna's tiny island. Tom saw with relief that the small fish flitted out of Arcta's path.

Get on my back! Arcta told Tom, turning his enormous muscular shoulders towards them.

"You first!" Tom told Elenna.
After jabbing one final stray fish
away with her arrow, Elenna
vaulted up on to Arcta's back.

As soon as Elenna was safe, Tom
leapt up beside her, clinging to
Arcta's shaggy fur as the Good
Beast set off. Tom's hands had
grown so numb by now, he could
hardly feel their pain. On the shore
ahead, Silver stopped pacing and
watched as Arcta carried Tom and
Elenna through the water with
long, steady strides. But before
they were halfway there, Tom felt
the giant's step falter. Arcta let out
a growl of surprise, and looking

down, Tom saw why.

The piranha fish were back, circling Arcta's legs, and as Tom watched, they drew together, melding into a new hideous shape – the huge, scaled body of a giant fish. The Beast gazed up at them from the depths with rows of eyes, dead and blank. They chilled Tom to the bone. But worse of all was her wide, smiling mouth, which was crammed with narrow teeth like needle-sharp shards of ice.

Devora is awake! Arcta cried.

5

DEVORA ATTACKS!

The fish-Beast surged towards them, her dagger-like teeth glinting and her scales rippling with light.

Biting back a cry of pain and clinging to Arcta with one injured hand, Tom drew his sword. Devora knifed closer, slicing through the water like an eel, but at the last possible moment, she changed course, sailing past Arcta with a flick of her tail. Tom frowned. *What is she up to?*

Cold, mirthless laughter answered him: Devora, speaking into his mind: *I hope you like the cold,* she hissed. The chilling sound was accompanied by the crackle of water freezing into ice. Frowning down into the lake, Tom made out glittering crystals forming in Devora's wake as she circled Arcta's legs.

The Good Beast swiped a fist at Devora, but she was too quick, diving out of range. With a furious bellow, Arcta started off once more, swinging his arms in wide arcs, smashing through the slushy ice forming around him. He managed a few lurching steps, then stopped again, mid-stride.

Tom saw the Good Beast could go no further – Devora had encased Arcta's massive body in a gleaming block of ice. The mammoth fish bobbed to the surface nearby, dead eyes fixed on Tom.

You will die... Tom heard her hiss, in a voice like an icy whip.

You will lie for ever, frozen in my lake...

Arcta must have heard Devora too, for he shook his head as if to clear his senses. *Do not worry, Master*, the Good Beast said. *The cold cannot harm me. I will not let you perish. I can throw you both to shore!*

He plucked Elenna from his back with his massive, hairy hand. Elenna yelped with surprise as the mountain giant drew back his arm and hurled her. Watching his friend soar over the frozen lake, Tom held his breath, then winced as she landed hard on the icy rock of the shore. Elenna rolled over, skidded to a stop then sat up with a groan.

Arcta reached out for Tom, but at the same moment, Devora hissed and dived deep below the ice.

"AARGH!" Arcta's body jack-knifed as he howled with pain. Devora must have snapped at his lower leg, where his body wasn't trapped in ice. Tom's hands, numb with cold and still half-bandaged, lost their grip on the Good Beast's pelt, and he tumbled on to the frozen surface, where he could see Devora's form darting though the inky water below, snapping for Arcta again. As her teeth bit deep into his hairy flesh, the Good Beast shuddered with agony. Tom could feel an echo of the Beast's pain though his ruby.

Tom forced himself to his feet, gathered his strength, then drove his sword, point first, deep into the ice.

Devora! I am your enemy, not Arcta!

The piranha-Beast whipped around and sped towards Tom. He drew his sword from the ice, expecting the surface to re-form as Devora swam below him, but instead the opposite happened. As the Beast circled tightly, the frozen lake above her began to turn to slush. Tom's boot plunged through the soft ice. *She can melt water as well as freeze it!* He managed to tug his boot free. He stumbled back a few paces, and was relieved to see

Devora following him, leaving Arcta behind, her passage marked by a line of melting ice.

Tom turned, and half-skidding, half-running, pounded over the frozen lake, putting as much distance between himself and Arcta as he could. Looking back, he saw a zigzag trail of slush where Devora followed behind him. *My plan's working!* But then, suddenly, the trail vanished. Tom stopped, scanning the ice, looking for any trace of the Beast.

CRASH! The ice right in front of him exploded upwards in broken shards and Devora's head jutted through. Tom reeled back, trying

to keep his footing, but the ice crumbled and he plunged once more into the freezing depths.

The terrible cold clamped shut about Tom's chest and skull, crushing the air from his lungs, driving waves of pain through his temples. As the freezing water filled his nose and mouth, Devora dived to meet him. Terror knifed through Tom's gut. Underwater, the Beast looked more hideous than ever. Her yellow eyes bulged hungrily, their monstrous gaze fixed on Tom. Devora smiled slowly, showing her gleaming dagger-like teeth, then opened her jaws impossibly wide, ready to devour her prey.

KARADIN'S REVENGE

Calling on the power of his golden gauntlets – hoping with every fibre of his being that their magical sword skills would work – Tom lifted his weapon and swiped for Devora just as she lunged for his throat. His blade raked along the side of her face, sending maroon

blood swirling out into the water.
With a furious hiss, the Beast
recoiled, then turned to face him
once more, her eyes narrowed with
hatred and her jaws gaping wide.

Tom's lungs were already
beginning to burn and his limbs

were stiff with cold. *I have to end this, fast.* He sent his sword lashing out, stabbing for Devora's throat. At the same moment she dived, snapping at his booted foot. Tom wrenched his leg out of the way just in time and sliced again, aiming for the Beast's shimmering scales, hoping to at least slow her down. Darting left, Devora evaded the strike, then came at Tom again. With his lungs screaming for air, Tom desperately tried to concentrate. His head throbbed and all he could see were Devora's glowing eyes, her jagged teeth, the hideous flesh of her scaled fish body. As she lunged for his chest, Tom struck out again, just raking the tip of his sword across her exposed underbelly. The wound was slight, but Devora writhed back in the water, hissing furiously, then exploded into a dazzling shoal of fish.

Tom swallowed hard. He was at the end of his strength, and now thousands of empty eyes stared back at him. Thousands of chomping teeth grinned hungrily, ready to tear him to shreds. He turned and swam as fast as he could for the surface. New points of pain erupted all over him as the fish bit into his arms and legs and held fast. Tom tried to shake the fish off, but they sank their teeth deeper, and now he could feel their added weight dragging him down. His lungs shuddered, throbbing with lack of air, and his head swam. *I'm going to drown!*

With no other option, Tom made one final desperate stand. Somersaulting in the water, he turned to face the shoal. The piranhas' blade-like teeth filled his view and their horrible bubbling chitter rang in his ears. Using both the enhanced sword skills of his magical gauntlets and the strength from his breastplate, Tom slashed his blade backwards and forwards in a frenzied attack, carving a path through the snapping fish and pushing himself up towards the surface. Spotting a gap in the thawing ice and using the last of his magical strength, Tom heaved himself out of the water.

The cold night air was barely warmer than the lake had been and the ice beneath him sucked any remaining warmth from his body. Tom shuddered, his teeth chattering so hard his vision blurred. Below him, in the lake, the piranha fish were swarming together, forming Devora the Death Fish once more. *I have to defeat her now, before I freeze!* Tom realised. *I need to find her weak spot.* He suddenly thought again of her soft-looking underbelly. How she had recoiled when his blade had scratched her rotten flesh. *Maybe that's it.* He was about to leap back into the depths when he heard a high, panicked voice.

"Tom!" Elenna cried. He turned to see her racing towards him over the ice. "The lake is thawing fast. The water is running towards Colton. We have to warn the villagers. Colton will flood! They'll all drown!"

Tom felt torn. He couldn't let innocent villagers perish – but he couldn't leave a Beast on the loose, either. He growled in frustration. "I have to stop Devora!" he shouted back.

"There will be other chances to defeat Karadin!" Elenna cried. "But if we don't act now, lives will be lost!"

Scanning the lake, Tom saw that almost the whole expanse was black water now. Arcta was still trapped, but other than his prison, only the broad section of ice that connected Tom to the shore and a few bobbing chunks remained. The surface of the lake had risen, and churning water streamed down the narrow gully leading to Colton.

"You're right," Tom said. "I'm coming." But, as he started towards Elenna, Devora's vile head thrust up through the ice again, right between them. The last big floe of ice shattered apart, separating him from Elenna, and Elenna from the shore. With a hiss of glee at the sight of new prey, Devora lunged toward Elenna. The Beast's sharp teeth slammed shut on the small ice-

sheet that was keeping Elenna afloat, biting off a chunk.

Tom glanced in the direction of Colton, thinking of all the villagers at home in their houses, unaware of their fate. *I must defeat Devora fast!* Tom realised. *If I fail, Elenna dies and so will the people of Colton!*

1

WOLF ON WATER

Elenna shrank back, balancing
right on the edge of what remained
of her tiny island as Devora worked
another chunk of ice free. Tom's
heart clenched in terror for his
friend, but she was too far away for
him to jump to her aid.

*Devora! Turn and face me! Or
are you too afraid?* he called to the

Beast. Devora, intent on her new
victim, kept chomping at the ice,
not even
glancing
his way.

Elenna
fumbled
with
her bow,
desperately
trying to
notch an
arrow,
but Tom
could see her hands were white
with cold and she was shivering too
hard. He wracked his brains, his
heart clenching each time Devora's

sharp teeth snapped closer to Elenna's feet. Suddenly, he heard an anguished howl. *Silver!* The wolf was watching his mistress from the shore, panting and whining in desperation. Silver ran his eyes over the water before him, taking in the choppy waves, the floating ice. Tom could almost see Silver's mind working. With a final glance at Elenna, the faithful wolf crouched and sprang... He leapt high, soaring over the inky water. Tom held his breath, watching helplessly as the wolf landed on a tiny island of ice and skidded. Silver scrabbled with his claws, stopping himself just before he tumbled into the lake.

"Silver, no! It's too dangerous!"
Elenna shouted. But, without
hesitation, Silver crouched and
jumped again, then again, springing
from ice floe to ice floe as he headed
towards her. Each perilous leap
brought him closer to Elenna. But,
as the wolf closed the gap, Tom saw
Devora's head snap around. Her
eyes narrowed with spite, she dived
away from Elenna, making a beeline
for the wolf.

"Silver! Watch out!" Elenna
screamed. Devora shot out of
the water just as Silver sprang.
Tom could hardly bear to watch.
The hideous Beast leapt high, her
enormous, scaled body almost

completely leaving the water and
her huge jaws reaching for Silver's
flank as
he arched
over her
head.

SNAP!
Devora's
sharp
teeth
slammed
shut only
a hand's
breadth
from

Silver's flesh. With a hiss of
frustration, the Beast plunged back
below the waves. Silver landed

safely. But not for long. Devora was already circling for another shot at him – which gave Tom an idea.

"Silver, stay!" Elenna commanded her wolf, frowning sternly at him, her face pale with worry. Silver looked back at her uncertainly. Tom could see he was unwilling to disobey a direct command – but he was still intent on reaching Elenna.

"Elenna!" Tom called. "I think I can use Silver to defeat the Beast. But I need you to count down, then call him to you, so we know when Devora will jump."

"It's too risky!" Elenna shouted back. "My hands are shaking too much! I'll miss my shot and...I just can't risk harming Silver!"

Tom shook his head. He had already thought of that. At his feet lay a single shard of shattered ice – as thick as his arm, and tapering to a wicked point. He lifted it to show Elenna. "I'll take the shot!" Tom called. "Trust me."

Elenna glanced at her wolf, crouched ready to follow her every command; then back at Tom. She looked torn. But she clenched her jaw and nodded. "I trust you," she said. "Let's do it!"

Tom steadied his shaking muscles, clenching his teeth to keep from shivering, and drew back his icy lance. *At least the cold of the shard*

has numbed the burns on my hands,
he thought. *Nothing must distract
me now.* In the lake below, Devora
circled Silver, her spines bristling,
her scales shimmering in the gloom.
Elenna's eyes were locked with
those of her wolf, who stood poised,
ready to leap.

"Stay," Elenna commanded,
then she started counting for Tom.
"Three... Two... One... Silver!
Come!" Elenna dropped to her
knees, throwing out her arms,
beckoning her wolf into them.
Silver's muscles bunched and he
leapt into the air, legs outstretched,
body arching... *SPLASH!* Below
Silver, the dark water parted in an

explosion of droplets and Devora burst up, her jaws stretched open as she surged towards the wolf. Time seemed to slow for Tom. He knew he had only one chance. Everything depended on him making this shot. Silver's life. His own. Elenna's. All the people of Colton. He waited until the Beast's pale, sickly-looking belly had just emerged from the depths, then threw the shard with all his strength. It

sang as it whooshed through the air,
catching the moon's rays, a blade
made of light...

THUNK! The shard sank deep
into Devora's flesh, so hard it drove
her body backwards through the
air. She landed with a dull *smack*
on the ice-floe Silver had just left,
flopped once like a trout in a net,
then lay still. An instant later, Silver
touched down at Elenna's feet, his
long claws finding purchase on the
ice and his tongue already licking
her cheek.

Elenna threw her arms around the
wolf, and buried her face in his fur.
Weak with relief, Tom sank down on
to the ice. *We did it!*

AVERTING THE FLOOD

While Elenna and Silver embraced, Tom watched the Beast closely, looking for any sign of life. Devora's scaled body looked limp and rotten with decay. Her eyes had a milky film and blood oozed from the wound in her side. She was defeated. Tom felt an instant change in the air – the frosty bite of the wind had gone, replaced by a balmy warmth. At his feet, the ice was already sheeny and wet, thawing fast.

Master! Tom heard Arcta call him through the power of his red jewel. He looked over to see the Good Beast breaking free from his melting prison, smashing it to slush with his arms and stamping his giant feet. *I am coming!* Arcta said. The mountain giant waded quickly towards Tom, scooped him up under one arm, and then crossed to Silver and Elenna. Before long, Arcta had deposited them all on the shore of the lake.

From here, though, it was only too clear how much danger Colton was in. Churning lake water poured in a furious flood through the narrow gully that led to the town.

"We have to help the people!" Elenna cried. Tom knew she was right. But how?

Leave it to me! Arcta said. The mighty cyclops strode towards the rocky gorge and started tearing huge chunks from the rock of the mountainside. Arcta tossed each boulder into the flowing meltwater, where they were swept along until they met a narrowing of the gorge. There, they halted. Before long, Arcta had created a thick dam

of stone. The lake water swelled,
filling the space, then stopped. The
people of Colton were safe!

Tom and Elenna hugged each
other in relief.

"Maybe now we can get warm!"
Elenna said. "And we can ask
someone in Colton to look at your
poor hands."

"And for some hot food!" Tom
said.

Silver circled them, his tail
wagging happily. Suddenly he
stopped, ears pricked. From across
the water came a spine-chilling
sound: an evil laughter. Out
towards the centre of the lake, a
single ice sheet remained. The body

of Devora was slumped on it: a stinking, rotten thing, devoid of life. Beside her, Karadin stood with his cloak thrown back, looking almost solid. He raised his skeleton hand. A flash of light shot from his ring, so bright Tom had to cover his eyes. When Tom could see again, Devora's rotting corpse

had gone. A few last wisps of black smoke flowed into Karadin's ring. Then the Evil ghost vanished too.

Tom sighed heavily as the last of the ice melted away into the lake, any feelings of victory he might have had dissolving with it.

"How do we beat Karadin if every defeat just makes him stronger?" Tom asked. "Especially when he seems to be taking my powers away in the process?"

Elenna stood with her hand resting on her wolf's back. "I don't know," she said. "But together, we will find a way, Tom! We always do!"

Tom squared his shoulders.

"You're right," he said. "I don't need magical powers to defeat Evil when I've got the power of friends on my side!"

THE END

CONGRATULATIONS, YOU HAVE COMPLETED THIS QUEST!

At the end of each chapter you were awarded a special gold coin.
The QUEST in this book was worth an amazing 8 coins.

Look at the Beast Quest totem picture opposite to see how far you've come in your journey to become

MASTER OF THE BEASTS.

The more books you read, the more coins you will collect!

Do you want your own
Beast Quest Totem?

1. Cut out and collect the coin below
2. Go to the Beast Quest website
3. Download and print out your totem
4. Add your coin to the totem

www.beastquest.co.uk

READ THE BOOKS, COLLECT THE COINS!
EARN COINS FOR EVERY CHAPTER YOU READ!

550+ COINS
MASTER OF THE BEASTS

410 COINS
HERO

350 COINS
WARRIOR

230 COINS
KNIGHT

180 COINS
SQUIRE

44 COINS
PAGE

8 COINS
APPRENTICE

550+
515
480
445
410
395
380
365
350
320
290
260
230
217
206
191
180
146
112
78
44
30
19
8

READ ALL THE BOOKS IN SERIES 27:
THE GHOST OF KARADIN!

Don't miss the next exciting Beast Quest book: RAPTEX THE SKY HUNTER!

Read on for a sneak peek...

THE EAGLE'S NEST

Tom was glad to see Storm still waiting for them as he, Elenna and Silver finally reached the bottom of the mountain. Storm lifted his head and let out a whinny of greeting but Tom was so exhausted he could barely summon a smile in return. It had been a long climb down from the village of Colton. Elenna's face was pale and covered in cuts and grazes. Tom had never seen her look so tired.

"Thank goodness we're back on level ground!" Elenna said. "I'd be happy to never see another mountain as long as I live!"

"I'm with you on that!" Tom said.

Beyond the grassy plains, the rising sun cast a fiery glow along the horizon. The sight gave Tom little joy. It marked yet another night passed without sleep...another night where victory seemed further away than ever on what might be their hardest Quest yet.

As Tom reached Storm, the stallion

nuzzled against him. Tom gave his
horse a quick rub and collapsed
on to the nearest boulder. Elenna
slumped down beside him and
Silver stretched out at their feet, his
flanks heaving. Tom felt a pang of
guilt. The wolf had scouted ahead
of them on their climb, and badly
needed rest – but there was no time
for that. Karadin, an ancient prince
and former Master of the Beasts, had
risen from the dead and was intent
on taking Avantia's throne. His
Evil ghost had already awoken two
fearsome Beasts. Tom and Elenna
had defeated them both, but Karadin
had absorbed the creatures' magical
essences and was now stronger than

ever, while Tom's own powers were waning.

Elenna took a long drink from her water bottle then poured some into a natural dip in the rock for Silver.

"So, where do we go now?" she asked Tom.

"Back up into the mountains, I fear," a faint voice murmured from nearby. Shading his eyes against the rising sun, Tom could just make out the pale, shimmering outline of Loris, Karadin's ghostly brother. The spirit had been guiding Tom and Elenna on their Quest so far, but like Tom, Loris's strength was failing as Karadin's grew. He was now like clear ice in water, barely visible at all.

"You know where Karadin is headed next?" Tom asked.

Loris nodded. "He is making his way towards a lonely mountain peak called the Eagle's Nest. Long ago, Karadin defeated a griffin-Beast there. He will seek to raise Raptex once more."

Tom shook his head, frustration welling inside him. "If we defeat Raptex, Karadin will steal his powers and become stronger than ever! How can we hope to win?"

"There's always hope," Elenna said. "We can do this, Tom!" Despite her bowed shoulders and the dark hollows beneath her eyes, her words were fierce. They gave Tom heart.

"Elenna is right," Loris said. "You can still intercept Karadin before he awakens Raptex. The mountain paths are treacherous, and always changing. They have become the final resting place of many unfortunate travellers. The way will not be easy, even for Karadin. You still have time."

Gazing back at the lofty heights they had just left, Elenna managed a weary smile. "Up again it is, then..." she said. But then she glanced at Silver and her smile changed to an anxious frown. Tom noticed that the wolf's ribs showed under his shaggy coat, and he looked older than when they had left King Hugo's palace. Storm needed a proper rest and a good meal too.

"Let's take the animals as far as Colton," Tom said. "We can stable them there and pick up supplies for the rest of the journey. Though they may not know it, the villagers owe us a debt of thanks!" Tom and Elenna had recently saved the mountain village from flooding – not to mention the terrifying piranha-Beast Devora.

Loris bowed his head. "I must bid you farewell for now," he said. "My life force is almost spent, but I wish you luck." With those words, Loris's shimmering form became more

translucent than ever, melting away.
He soon vanished into the morning
air.

Tom and Elenna set off at once,
trudging back up the narrow
mountain path with Storm and
Silver behind them. The sun
climbed higher in the blue sky as
they travelled. It beat against Tom's
shoulders, and coupled with an
icy wind, meant he was soon both
sweating and chilled to the bone.

By the time the squat stone
buildings of Colton came into sight,
Tom's legs ached so much he could
hardly move them and hunger
gnawed at his gut. A sudden whiff
of roasting meat on the breeze made

him quicken his pace.

As they neared the small town, he saw that bright awnings filled the village square.

"Market day!" Elenna said.

Tom nodded. "We're in luck. We should be able to get everything we need!"

After leaving Silver at the outskirts of town, Tom and Elenna led Storm up on to the rocky plateau that housed the village. But, to Tom's dismay, it soon became clear that Colton had known better days.

Read
RAPTEX THE SKY HUNTER
to find out what happens next!

Don't miss the
thrilling new series
from Adam Blade!

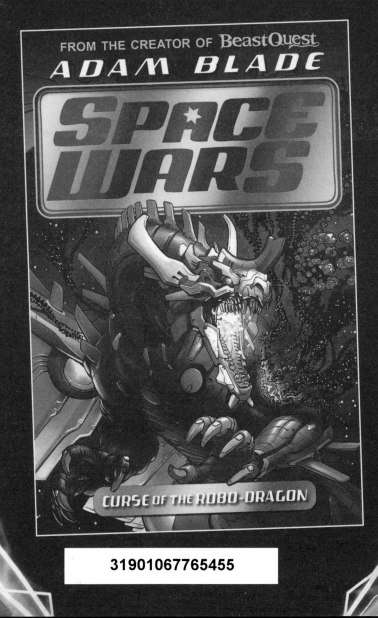

31901067765455